W9-AOR-538

The
Scruffy
Puppy

Read these other books by Holly Webb:

Lost in the Snow
Lost in the Storm
Sam the Stolen Puppy
Alfie All Alone
Max the Missing Puppy
Sky the Unwanted Kitten
Ginger the Stray Kitten
Harry the Homeless Puppy
Timmy in Trouble
Ellie the Homesick Puppy
Jess the Lonely Puppy
Buttons the Runaway Puppy
Oscar's Lonely Christmas
Alone in the Night
Misty the Abandoned Kitten
Lucky the Rescued Puppy
Whiskers the Lonely Kitten
Lucy the Littlest Puppy
Smudge the Stolen Kitten
Cookie the Deserted Puppy
The Snow Bear
The Kidnapped Kitten
The Frightened Kitten

The Scruffy Puppy

Holly Webb

Illustrated by Sophy Williams

SCHOLASTIC INC.

No part of this publication may be reproduced, stored in a retrieval system, or transmitted in any form or by any means, electronic, mechanical, photocopying, recording, or otherwise, without written permission of the publisher. For information regarding permission, write to Stripes Publishing, an imprint of Magi Publications, 1 The Coda Centre, 189 Munster Road, London SW6 6AW, United Kingdom.

ISBN 978-0-545-80326-7

Text copyright © 2014 by Holly Webb
Illustrations copyright © 2014 by Sophy Williams

All rights reserved. Published by Scholastic Inc., 557 Broadway, New York, NY 10012.
SCHOLASTIC and associated logos are trademarks and/or registered trademarks of Scholastic Inc.

12 11 10 9 8 7 6 5 4 3 2   15 16 17 18 19/0

Printed in the U.S.A.   40
First Scholastic printing, March 2015

Chapter One

Bella couldn't help doing a kind of hopping dance as they went up the steps at the front of the animal shelter. She was just too excited to walk normally. She had been waiting so long for this day. It had been weeks and weeks since Mom and Dad had first started talking seriously about getting a dog, and before that Bella had been trying to persuade them for *years*.

Still, they were really here, walking into Redlands Animal Shelter to find a dog who could be their very own.

"What kind of dog do you think we'll get?" she asked suddenly, turning around on the top step, and looking at her mom and dad, and Tom, her older brother. They were all following behind her as she had run ahead of them from the car. Bella had wanted to ask this question— and lots of others—ever since Mom had told them about the trip to the animal shelter earlier in the week. But she hadn't quite dared. What if they couldn't decide on a favorite breed and gave up on the whole idea? Even now, she glanced anxiously from Mom to Dad to Tom, wondering what they would say. She'd been thinking about it a lot herself—trying to decide what her absolute favorite, best, loveliest kind of dog would be.

She hadn't thought about much else for weeks, actually. Her friend Megan had started to roll her eyes every time Bella mentioned dogs at school, or suggested going to the library to look at dog books again. And Mr. Peters, their teacher, had told Bella to stop daydreaming at least three times. On the other hand, he had given her a star and two class points for her poem about dogs. So it sort of evened out.

But even after all that, Bella still hadn't decided what her top dog was. She knew they were getting their dog from the shelter because buying a dog from a breeder would be very expensive, and Mom and Dad really wanted to give a home to a dog who didn't have one, as well. So in a way, it was good that she hadn't set her heart on one particular breed, because the chances of that exact breed being at the shelter were probably small. Still, wasn't it a little strange that she couldn't decide what her favorite dog really was, when she could choose from any that she liked? She knew what the problem was—it was just that she liked them *all* . . .

"If there was every sort of dog at the shelter, what would your favorite be?" she asked her mom. "I know it won't be there," she added hurriedly. "I'm just interested."

Mom smiled at her. "I'd been wondering when you'd ask that. I was a little surprised that you hadn't been on the computer, looking at dog websites and figuring out exactly what sort of dog you'd like."

Bella gave her a little embarrassed smile. "That's just what I have been doing!" she admitted. "But I can't decide!"

Mom ruffled Bella's hair as she opened the door to the shelter's reception area. "If I could have any dog in the world, I'd like something little and cute. Maybe a dachshund."

"Is that a wiener dog?" Tom asked suspiciously. "I don't want a wiener dog. My friends would laugh. Something big would be cool." He grinned. "I really like those big hairy things."

Bella rolled her eyes. "Great description. Which big hairy things?"

"You know. The ones in the bus ads."

"Oh! An Old English Sheepdog!"

Bella nodded excitedly. "They're beautiful."

"Sorry, you two." Dad shook his head at Bella and Tom. "I don't think there'll be an Old English Sheepdog here, or even a dachshund. I would think most of the dogs will be strays. Mixed breeds, probably."

Bella nodded. Mom was over by the reception desk now, explaining that they'd like to look at dogs for adoption. Bella was so happy, she couldn't keep still. She had to keep talking, or she might burst with excitement. "What kind of dog would you like, Dad?"

"Hmm." Dad frowned. "I'd like something big. I like the idea of taking a dog when I go running."

Tom snorted. "So, a greyhound then."

Their dad was really tall and he liked to go on long runs. He had even run a marathon before—they'd all gone to cheer him on.

Bella shook her head. "I don't know about a greyhound, Dad. I'm not sure they could keep up with you. They're more about going super-fast, but only for a short time. And anyway, if there was a greyhound here, it might be an ex-racing dog." She frowned, and stood still for a minute. "And they're really sad. The owners just dump them when they can't race anymore, and they've never had a real home, or been looked after. They all have terrible teeth, because the owners never took real care of them. I read about one who had to have all his teeth taken out."

Dad sighed. "I think quite a few of the dogs here might have sad stories, Bella. We just have to think that at least we're going to give one of them a home." He put an arm around her shoulders. "So, what do you think? Big hairy dog? Tiny little fluffy thing?"

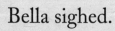

Bella sighed.

"I just don't know! I keep trying to imagine myself with different kinds of dogs, but I like all of them . . ." She smiled up at her dad. "When we see them for real, it'll be different, won't it? We'll know which is the perfect dog for us. I'm sure we will."

"How are we ever going to choose?" Bella said helplessly. There were so many dogs, and most of them were really excited to see visitors. They jumped up from their beds, and hurried over to the wire netting in the front of the pens, scrabbling like crazy, and begging to be petted, loved, taken home. There were just a few who didn't bother getting up, and Bella thought that they were even sadder. Those dogs must have been at the shelter so long that they knew it was no use. No one was ever going to want them. Their hopeless eyes made her want to cry.

The worst thing was that she could see that her family couldn't take them, either. They were mostly old, and didn't look like they'd want to go for runs with Dad, or play around in the yard with her and Tom. But she wished she could be the one to make them happy.

"Are you OK?" One of the center staff stopped next to her, smiling. She had a badge on that said "Jo—Manager."

Bella gulped. "Yes. I guess. It's just so sad. Some of the dogs look like they've given up."

Jo sighed. "I know. But it's not completely hopeless, you know. We do find almost all of them homes in the end, even though it can take a long time. Older dogs can be great, gentle pets." She smiled at Bella. "I would think you and your family would like something a bit bouncier, though."

"Yes, please." Bella nodded. "I don't really mind what breed or anything. I just want to have a dog of our own."

Jo looked at her thoughtfully. "Did you see Sid?"

Bella frowned. "I don't think so. Is he up there somewhere?" She pointed farther down the line of pens, where her dad and Tom were crouched down looking in at a big Boxer, who was barking as if he would burst with excitement.

"No, no, you've passed him. Here." Jo led Bella back a couple of pens, and stopped so she could peer in.

The basket was in the corner of the pen, and all Bella could see was a fuzzy brown-and-white back.

Jo chuckled. "He could sleep forever, this one. But when he's awake, he's a cutie. Well . . ." she paused. "He *is* cute. But he's not exactly the best-looking dog in the world. I have to admit, most people pass him over. But I think he's sweet. I'd take him home myself if I didn't have four cats already."

"Has he been here for a while?" Bella asked, crouching down to look at the brown-and-white furry lump in the basket.

"About, um, four months." Jo sighed. "He's starting to give up, which is so sad. I think he sleeps so much because he really hates being here. He's sweet and affectionate with the staff, but he wants space to run in. A little time in the exercise yard just isn't enough."

"My dad really wants a dog who could go running with him," Bella said hopefully. "And my mom just wants a dog who isn't too huge. Sid doesn't look that big. Is he?" She wrapped her fingers around the wire, staring in and wishing Sid would wake up. The fuzzy white back twitched and wriggled a bit.

"No, he's some kind of terrier mix. Medium-sized, but with longish legs. And even though he's still very young, I don't think he'll get much bigger."

"You mean he's a puppy?" Bella asked excitedly. She hadn't thought they'd be able to get a young dog. Mom and Dad had explained that most of the dogs at the shelter would already have had one owner.

Jo smiled. "Well, let's just say he's a teenager."

"Oh, I wish he'd wake up and come and see me." Bella sighed.

Inside the pen, Sid heard the voices. The nice one, who always pet him even more than the others when she brought his food. She always scratched his ears, and chatted, and he could tell she liked him. She was talking to someone that he hadn't heard before, though. His ears twitched thoughtfully, and he wondered if it was one of the people who took dogs away. Someone had taken the young terrier in the opposite pen only yesterday. But even though people looked into his enclosure, they didn't usually want the door opened so they could meet him. He'd stopped bothering to wag his tail and give them hopeful looks. None of them really seemed to see him anyway.

His ears flattened and he wriggled around in his basket a bit. He would go back to sleep, until it was time for food.

"Oh! I thought he was going to wake up!" the young girl said.

The voice sounded sad, and Sid's ears pricked up again. He couldn't help it. He glanced over his shoulder and saw the nice woman there with a girl beside her, crouched by the wire and staring at him.

"He *is* awake!" the girl said excitedly. "Oh, how could anyone not find him cute? He's gorgeous! Look at his beautiful ears!"

The brown-and-white dog looked like a sort of wiry-haired terrier, but his frizzy ears had come from somewhere else entirely. Maybe a spaniel, or something little and fluffy like a Papillon? The ones with the ears like butterflies? Or maybe a poodle? Bella wasn't sure, but she loved them. They made him look like a dog who'd been put together from bits. As he got up and came cautiously toward them, she saw that he had a feathery tail, too. He walked over to the wire slowly, and his tail began to wiggle from side to side.

"Hello!" Bella breathed. "Oh, aren't you sweet?" She glanced up at Jo. "Is it OK to put my fingers through the wire? So I can pet him?" she asked.

"Sure, as long as you're gentle—Sid's very friendly," Jo answered.

Bella slipped her fingers through the netting, and giggled as Sid came closer and licked at them curiously. "That tickles! Hello, sweetheart." Carefully, slowly, she reached her fingers around

to rub under his chin. All the dogs she'd met before loved that. It seemed that Sid did, too. He closed his eyes and sighed blissfully.

"Please can we open the pen? So I can meet him for real?" Bella said.

Jo smiled at her. "Shouldn't we see what your mom and dad think first?" she said.

"Oh! Oh, yes, I forgot. I'll get them! I'm sure they'll love him. I'll be back in a minute, Sid." And Bella jumped up, hurrying away between the pens. The lady at reception had told them not to run, in case it upset the dogs, but she just couldn't help going fast.

Sid sighed and his tail dropped down. His ears sagged as well and he turned to trail back to his basket. It had been stupid to think that the girl had liked him. She had fussed over him and rubbed his chin in just his favorite place, but then she had vanished.

"Hey . . ." Jo called gently. "She's only gone to find her mom and dad. She's coming back. Sid . . . Don't be sad, my sweetie."

But Sid had gone back to his basket and curled up determinedly. He wasn't listening.

Chapter Two

"Well, he doesn't look very friendly," Mom said doubtfully.

"Oh, but he is! Well, he was . . ." Bella pleaded. "You tell them," she said, turning to Jo.

"He's a sweet dog, but he's been here a while and he hasn't been adopted," Jo explained. "Some dogs stop bothering to try and say hello to everyone."

"Oh . . ." Bella saw her mom's face crumple a little. Her mom was just as sappy as she was. A dog who thought he'd never have a real home was making them both want to cry.

"We could at least open the pen and meet him, couldn't we?" Bella asked, fixing her eyes on her mom.

"Oh, yes." Mom nodded.

Sid was still in his basket, but his ears were twitching frantically. There were lots of people outside his pen now—he could hear them. Were they talking about him? He popped his head up a fraction and darted a glance across the pen.

"Aw, look at him!" Bella's mom laughed. "Look at those ears!"

"Exactly!" Bella beamed at her.

"Isn't he a bit . . . scruffy-looking?" Dad said, coming up behind them with Tom.

Bella glared at him. "He's beautiful!"

"He does have a lovely personality," Jo put in as she opened the pen. "Very friendly, and he likes lots of exercise. Bella said you like to run? He'd really love that. He's got nice long legs . . ."

Dad smiled. "Let's meet him."

Sid stood up in his basket, his tail waving uncertainly back and forth. They were definitely getting him out! His tail wagged faster and faster, and when Jo called, "Sid! Sid, here boy!" he shot out of the basket so fast he skidded over the tiled floor, and almost crashed into Dad's feet.

"Hello!" Dad laughed. "All right, you're excited, aren't you!" He rubbed Sid's huge feathery ears, while Bella scratched him under the chin again. Sid stood there, practically dribbling with pleasure.

"What do you think, Tom?" Mom asked.

Tom was grinning. "He's great. Dad, you know he's about to drool on your sneakers?" Tom crouched down by Sid and pet his back. "He's a weird mix, isn't he. Short fur and fluffy ears. But he's really friendly."

Bella sighed happily, and Sid looked up at her with shy black eyes. "I told you, didn't I," she whispered as Dad stood up and began to talk to Jo about dates for bringing Sid home with them. "I said they'd love you, and I was right!"

"He's so sweet," Bella told Megan as they put their coats away. She'd been waiting for her friend by the gate, but Megan hadn't arrived until just before the bell. Bella should have known—it was the same every morning—but she'd been desperate to tell Megan about Sid.

"The lady from the shelter's coming over after school to see the house —"

"What for?" Megan asked, sounding surprised.

"Oh, to make sure it's a good home for a dog. That we've got a yard, and no young children, things like that."

"I'd have thought they couldn't be that picky." Megan shrugged. "If they're just stray dogs."

"Well, they've got to find them nice homes," Bella pointed out, feeling a bit hurt. "Or they'll only end up back at the shelter again, won't they."

"Hmm, I guess so. Did you do that math homework?"

"Yes." Bella was about to start telling Megan how beautiful Sid's ears were, but her friend was already hurrying out of the cloakroom. Bella sighed. Maybe she was talking about Sid a little too much. But how could she stop talking about him when he was so wonderful?

The home visit went well, even though Bella was really nervous. She'd been certain that Jo would find something awful about their house, and say that they couldn't bring Sid home after all.

But Jo seemed to think they'd be great dog owners, especially as Mom worked from home. Bella had shown her a leaflet about dog-training classes, which she'd picked up at the place where she went for dance class, and Jo had beamed at her.

"Great! You sound as though you're taking it all really seriously. I think Sid shouldn't be too hard to train. He's very good-natured, and he already knows how to sit and walk to heel."

Jo had also told them a little bit of Sid's story. He'd been found abandoned as a puppy, stuffed into a cardboard box at the dump. Mom had cried when Jo told them that, and Bella had felt like crying, too. How could anyone be so cruel? It had made all of them—Mom, Dad, Bella, and

Tom—determined to make sure that Sid had the best home ever after such an awful start.

Jo had arranged that they could come and pick Sid up on the weekend— just a week after they'd first seen him. It wasn't really all that long to wait, but for Bella, it seemed as though the week lasted forever. She dashed out of school on Friday afternoon with just the quickest, "Bye! Have a nice weekend!" to Megan. She and her mom were meeting Tom up the road at his school. Then they were all going to the pet shop to choose a basket and the other things that Sid would need once they brought him home.

By the time they got to the shelter at nine o'clock on Saturday morning,

Bella had already been up for hours, and she was buzzing with excitement. Today was the day! They were really going to be bringing Sid home.

"I've been making a big fuss over him," Jo said, smiling. "He was a bit sad when you left last weekend—he'll be so happy to see you again."

Bella nodded. She'd been worrying that Sid wouldn't understand they were coming back to get him.

"Dad and I will look over the paperwork," Mom suggested to Bella and Tom. "Why don't you two go and see Sid?"

"Ah, is that a new collar and leash for him?" Jo smiled. "Let's go and get him and put them on. Then we can bring him out here to your mom and dad."

Bella gulped excitedly.

Tom fumbled at the clasp on the collar, undoing it so they were ready to give it to Sid. "This is so cool," he muttered, nudging Bella. "Our own dog!"

"I can't believe it's really happening," Bella whispered back as they followed Jo down to the pens.

But it was. Sid was there, sitting hopefully by his door, as if he'd heard their voices. When he saw them his tail beat slowly back and forth, and he glanced from Bella to Tom and back to Bella again, as though he wasn't quite sure it was really happening either.

"He's so lovely," Bella murmured, choking up a little bit.

"Don't start crying!" Tom rolled his eyes. "You're as bad as Mom! This is a good thing, Bella! Hey, Sid," he added in a gentle voice. "Look what we brought for you." He held out the leash, and Sid's slowly wagging tail suddenly went about ten times faster.

Jo laughed. "He loves his walks. Or his runs, I should say." She opened the pen door and let Tom slip inside to fuss over Sid, and then put the collar on.

"It looks so nice," Bella said proudly. The collar was a nice blue one that she'd chosen, with a matching leash. Mom had even had their phone number put on the little bone-shaped tag already.

Tom grinned at her, and passed over the leash. "You can take him, Bella. You chose him, after all."

Bella's fingers were shaking as she took the leash, and Sid stared up at her hopefully. His tail was still wagging at top speed. "Are you coming with us, Sid?" she murmured.

"Want to go home?"

Sid sat in his comfy, padded basket, watching solemnly as Bella showed him all the toys they'd bought.

"And look, this is a squeaky bone!" She squeaked it for him and laid it down to join the line with all the others.

"Bella went a bit overboard at the pet shop," her mom said, leaning down to stroke his ears. "This is enough for about three dogs, isn't it, Sid!"

Sid recognized his name, and wagged his tail a bit, even though he didn't know what they were talking about.

"I hope he's OK," Bella murmured worriedly. "He's so quiet."

"A new home is a lot to get used to, I would think," Mom pointed out. "Give him some time."

Sid looked at Bella, her straight blond hair falling over her face as she crouched down to arrange the toys for him again. He liked her. He liked her a lot. As she came close, he leaned out of the basket and gave her cheek a sweeping, wet lick.

Bella collapsed backward, giggling, and Sid followed her, planting his hairy white paws on her tummy so he could lick her again.

"Uuuugggh, Sid!" But Bella put her arms around his neck and hugged him. "You silly dog," she told him lovingly, and Sid licked her one more time.

Chapter Three

"Hi! Megan, is that you?" Bella said excitedly into the phone. "We've got him! Sid's at home with us—we brought him home yesterday! Do you want to come over and meet him? Mom says you can." Bella waited expectantly for a voice at the other end, sure that Megan would jump at the chance.

"Actually, sorry, Bella, I can't."

"Oh . . ." Bella didn't know what to say—she was really disappointed. Megan sounded as if she was excited about something, though. There was a bubbly sort of sound to her voice, as if she had a secret.

"Do you have some news?" Bella asked curiously.

"Yes—we got a dog, too! We got her yesterday. She's a spaniel and we're calling her Coco." Megan's words spilled over each other, she was so eager to tell Bella her news.

For just a moment, Bella felt a bit annoyed—getting a dog was her special thing. She had been wanting one forever. And now Megan had a dog, too, just like that. She knew that Megan's mom and dad gave her lots of things—whatever she wanted really, because she was an only child and they worried that she was lonely. But why a dog? Bella hadn't even thought Megan liked dogs all that much.

"I didn't know you wanted a dog," she said quietly, trying not to let the things she was thinking show in her voice.

"You kept talking about how great it would be. So—I thought maybe you were right. I begged Dad, and he took me to choose a puppy yesterday."

"Right away? You didn't have to have a home visit or anything?"

"Of course not!" Megan laughed. "Coco came from a breeder, not a shelter. She's a pedigree dog. She was *very* expensive," she added proudly.

"Oh . . ." Bella frowned. Sid hadn't been expensive. They'd paid a donation to the shelter, to help take care of the other dogs, but that was all . . . Bella chewed her lip worriedly, and then gasped in surprise as a warm weight settled on her feet.

Sid stared up at her lovingly, and Bella giggled and tickled his tummy with her bare toes. She was being stupid. It was great that Megan had a dog, too. "Maybe we can all go to the park this afternoon!" she suggested excitedly. "Sid and Coco could make friends."

"I'll ask Mom," Megan said. "Hold on."

Bella waited patiently as she heard her off in the background, talking to her mom. A few moments later, Megan came back to the phone.

"Bella? I forgot, we can't yet," she said. "The breeder said we ought to give her time to adjust to being at home with us. I think it's silly, but Mom says we have to."

"Oh! OK. Well, I'm sure she's right."

"I guess so. Anyway, bring a photo of Sid to school, OK? I'll bring one of Coco."

"All right." Bella put the phone back in its cradle on the kitchen windowsill, and reached down to run her hand over Sid's soft ears. "I don't care that you weren't expensive," she whispered. "I think you're perfect."

"Finally!" Tom put his head around the door. "I thought you were never getting off the phone. Mom says we can all go for a—" He eyed Sid carefully and said the last word in a whisper. "Walk."

Even though Tom had whispered the words, Sid still jumped around in a complete circle, ears flapping, his helicopter tail practically lifting him off the ground.

"Well, someone's excited." Bella giggled. "Come on then!"

Bella's house was near a small park with a little children's playground and a stretch of grass. There was a bigger one a little farther away, but they decided not to go too far for the first walk.

Bella, Tom, and Sid were so excited that it was hard to remember about walking to heel. All three of them just wanted to run. It seemed mean to make Sid walk slowly when it was the first time he'd had a real walk in forever. The shelter had told them that they used volunteers to take the dogs for walks, but there were never enough to take all the dogs out.

Sid could smell the park—the scent of grass and other dogs, and space to run in. But he did his best to walk next to Bella, the way he'd been taught.

"He's being so good," Dad said, sounding a bit surprised. "I was expecting him to be pulling your arm off, Bella."

Bella nodded. "You're such a good boy. Good *boy*, Sid."

Sid shook his frizzy ears happily and nosed at Bella's leg. The park was really close now. He stopped short as they came up to the gate, gazing at the biggest open space he'd ever seen.

"I think he's too excited to move," Mom said, laughing. "Go on in, Bella. See if he wants to go for a run."

Bella nodded and handed the leash to Tom—she didn't want to, but he'd let her take Sid all the way there, so it was his turn. She walked off backward, calling gently to Sid. "Here, Sid! Come on! Let's run!"

And a white streak of excited dog raced out across the grass toward Bella, with Tom galloping at the end of his leash.

When Bella arrived at school on Monday morning, for once Megan had actually gotten there on time.

She was sitting on one of the playground benches near the door to their classroom, with an admiring crowd gathered around her.

Bella hurried over, eager to talk about the dogs, and how much fun it was to be an owner at last. But it wasn't easy to get a word in. Megan had a lot of photos, in a special holder covered in paw prints. She was happily showing them off to all the girls in their class. Bella peered over. Coco did look very, very sweet. She was a little golden cocker spaniel, with huge dark-brown eyes and very curly ears. She was wearing a collar made of pink sparkly stones that looked a little big for her in the photo that Bella could see.

"I've got three little coats for her and four different collars," Megan was saying airily. "She's so pretty, she looks perfect in everything. Oh, hi, Bella! Look, this is Coco!"

"She's so cute." Bella nodded. She could see more of the photos now—one for every different collar and outfit, and quite a few with Coco lined up next to the stuffed animals on Megan's bed.

That's what Coco's like, Bella thought suddenly. *One of Megan's stuffed animals.* Bella couldn't say that, though. Not without upsetting Megan. And besides, she felt mean. But she did feel sorry for Coco—she must have been changed in and out of coats and collars all weekend. A puppy wasn't a doll for dressing up.

"She's got a pedigree, too," Megan said proudly. "Lots of her relatives have won prizes—one of them's a Supreme Grand Champion. Coco's really called Golden Daydream of Melton."

Bella giggled. She couldn't help it— it was such a silly-sounding name. But Megan glared at her crossly. "Did you bring a photo of your dog?" she demanded.

"Yes," Bella murmured, suddenly

wondering if she wanted to show Megan right now, with all these girls around. Especially when they'd just been looking at super-pretty Coco. They might not think Sid was very special. In fact, they might think he was downright scruffy.

"Go on, Bella. We want to see! Is your puppy a spaniel, too?" Lara asked. She and Chloe hung around with Megan and Bella a lot, but sometimes Bella wished they didn't. Lara could be mean, and Chloe just giggled and went along with everything that Lara said.

"Yeah, show us!" Chloe said now, giggling.

Bella looked down at her school bag, which was a little chewed around the edges. She'd left it on one of the chairs in the kitchen and Sid had obviously wanted a midnight snack. Mom had said that they'd better not leave anything out in the kitchen overnight from now on. The photo was in the front pocket, but she didn't really want to get it out. What if they laughed at Sid?

"Come on!" Lara huffed. "I bet she doesn't even have a dog at all. She's just making it up to copy Megan."

"I am not!" Bella said furiously. If anything it was the other way around. She glared at Lara and Megan. "I told you about Sid last week, and how we were going to adopt him from the animal shelter. He's a mix of lots of breeds."

"Oh, so he doesn't have a kennel name like Coco does?" Megan asked.

Bella eyed her. Megan knew that Sid didn't have a fancy kennel name. She was just trying to show Bella up, to look good in front of Lara and Chloe and the others.  Bella pulled the photo of Sid from her bag, and held it out.

Lara snorted. "What is *that*?"

"That's Sid," Bella said through her teeth. "He's probably a sort of terrier mix."

"Mixed with a mop?" Lara said, nudging Megan and snickering. "Bella, that's the oddest dog I've ever seen!"

Bella felt hot tears pricking the back

of her eyes and blinked them away. Chloe and some of the others laughed, but for a second, Bella thought she saw Megan look uncomfortable.

"Isn't it odd?" Lara said, nudging Megan again, and this time Megan nodded and snickered.

"Well, I think he looks really sweet," someone said behind Bella. She whirled around gratefully, wondering who it was. Not many people would stand up to Lara when she was picking on someone.

It was the new girl, Sarah, and she was peering over Bella's shoulder at the photo of Sid. "His ears are cute," she added. "Maybe there's some poodle in him."

"Yes," Bella agreed gratefully. She

hardly knew Sarah—she'd only started at their school this semester. In fact, she wasn't sure she'd ever spoken to her before. But now she wanted to hug her. "I thought so, too. And he's a really fast runner. So maybe some whippet, too."

"You're really lucky to have a dog." Sarah sighed. "We live in an apartment so we can't have one."

"Did anyone ask for your opinion?" Lara snapped. "And who cares if you live in an apartment? We certainly don't!"

Bella looked apologetically at Sarah. Sometimes, Lara was totally horrible. But it was just easier to be friends with her than not . . .

Sarah went pink and started to walk away.

Bella watched her for a second, hesitating, and then grabbed Sarah's arm. "Hey, do you want to come over and meet Sid? On Friday maybe?" she asked.

She could feel Lara's and Megan's eyes boring into her back—it was as if their eyes were burning holes in her back. But she didn't care. They were both being mean, and Sarah sounded like she knew about dogs and would be fun to talk to.

Sarah just gazed at her in amazement, and then she nodded. "Yes, please. I'll have to ask my mom, but I'd love to come and meet him."

A few of the girls who were gathered around the bench whispered and muttered, and Bella caught a couple of doubtful glances aimed at Lara. It was as though the others thought she was being too nasty as well.

"My dad says we can enter Coco in a dog show!" Megan said suddenly behind them, trying to get everyone's attention back. "And she'll probably win, because she's really well-bred."

"Not like that thing Bella's calling a dog." Lara snickered.

Bella dug her fingernails into her palms. She was sick of Lara being mean, and Megan sucking up to her. "Actually, Sid's going to be in a show, too!" she snapped at Megan.

Then Bella stomped away, wishing she hadn't said anything. She could hear them all snickering, and there was no way Sid was going to be in a dog show—after all, where would she ever find one to enter him in?

Chapter Four

Sid prowled backward and forward in front of the door, stopping occasionally to sniff the faint breeze that came wafting in around the sides. Then he flopped down on the doormat with a huge sigh.

When would they be back? Bella and Tom had been away all day, and even though their mom had been around, she had been sitting quietly and not wanting to play. She would pet him if he whined at her, but then she went back to the pieces of paper she was working on. She had gotten up to let him out into the yard a couple of times, and she had taken him for a quick walk at lunch, but she hadn't really played. And then she had gone out. He was bored.

Then his ears pricked up. He could hear footsteps! He jumped to his feet and snuffled hopefully at the bottom of the door. Yes! It was Bella—he could hear her voice. Sid let out a delighted yap, and then he heard Bella, excited and running.

"Listen, Tom! He heard us coming. Hi, Sid!"

Sid barked loudly, racing around the hallway so fast he nearly knocked over the basket of scarves and hats by the front door. When the door opened—carefully, because Bella's mom suspected he was probably right behind it—he whirled and bounced around their feet, jumping up and squeaking with joy.

"I don't think he missed us," Tom said in a pretend-sad voice, making Bella laugh.

"It's so nice to see you," Bella murmured, crouching down and hugging Sid. "I can't believe I let Megan and the others make me think you weren't perfect."

It didn't take long for Sid to get used to the pattern of living with a family. Even though there were boring parts when Bella and Tom were away for the whole day at school, he could usually doze through those, or chew his toys. The walks made up for the slow times.

After the first couple of days, Bella

and Tom were allowed to take him out on their own after school. Mom and Dad said it was all right, as long as they stayed together and Tom took his phone—he had gotten one when he'd gone to middle school. When they got back, Sid would take a nap while Bella did her homework, and then they'd go out into the yard and practice training.

Bella was determined that Sid was going to be the most beautifully trained dog ever. She had even bought a book about it with her allowance, and in a couple of weeks they were going to start classes. Somehow, because he was a little scruffy-looking, Bella felt that people who met Sid might think he was badly behaved. So she was determined to do her absolute best to make sure that he *wasn't*.

Luckily, Sid really seemed to like the training. Especially the delicious dog treats that Bella used as rewards. She was trying to teach him to sit and stay until she called him, and he was getting really good at it. Or at least he was while Bella was looking at him. If she turned her back, he would start to creep very, very slowly toward her and then as soon as she turned around again, he would look all innocent.

Bella wanted to teach Sid to come when he was called, so that she could safely let him off the leash in the park. But she had decided to wait until the training classes for that one. She didn't quite trust herself to teach Sid on her own. What if he disappeared off to the other end of the park and wouldn't come back? Or—even worse—he ran out through the gates onto the road?

As much as she loved the training sessions, it was their morning walks that were Bella's favorite. She and Dad had to get up extra early to take Sid out before breakfast, but she didn't mind. It was lovely—there weren't many people around, and they could use Sid's special extending leash, so he could run all across the park. Dad had warned Bella that the walks might not be so much fun in winter when it was cold and dark, but she couldn't imagine not wanting to take Sid out. He loved walks so much and that made her happy.

"Still not bored with getting up early?" Dad asked Bella on Thursday as she let out a massive yawn on the way to the park.

"No!" Bella shook her head firmly. "I'm just sleepy. I love the walks."

"How's Megan getting on with her new dog?" Dad asked.

Bella nibbled her bottom lip. She didn't want to tell Dad that she'd hardly spoken to Megan since Monday. They had been best friends since they'd started school, and even though Megan annoyed her sometimes, Bella missed her. And she didn't really feel like talking about it. "She's fine."

"Ooooh, watch out, Bella. Another dog coming," her dad said suddenly. "Want me to take the leash?"

Bella shook her head. "No, I'm sure he'll be good. Heel, Sid." She pressed the button on the extending leash that made it go short again and patted her leg, calling encouragingly to Sid. He pattered over to her at once, tail wagging. He'd seen the other dog and he wanted to sniff at him, but Bella was calling.

"Oh, good boy!" Bella rubbed his ears and drew him over to the side of the path so that the lady with the dog—a huge Weimaraner—could get past. But instead, the lady stopped and smiled.

"Have you just gotten your dog? I haven't seen you out walking him before."

"Yes, we adopted him from Redlands, the shelter," Dad explained.

"He's very sweet! And so well behaved. It's lovely to see you training him to walk well with you," she added to Bella. "You're obviously working really hard with him. Have a nice morning!"

And she walked on, leaving Dad and Bella staring at each other proudly. Then they both started telling Sid how fabulous he was. "You little star, Sid! Did you hear what she said?"

Sid stared up at them, wondering what all the fuss was about. All he'd done was stand still . . .

Chapter Five

Bella had chatted with Sarah a few more times since the new girl had stuck up for her on Monday with Megan and the others. But to be honest, she wasn't really looking forward to bringing her home for dinner. Mom had been fine with it—she'd said it was good to have lots of different friends, and that it must have been hard for Sarah to start a new school in the middle of the year.

Bella knew that was all true, but it didn't make Sarah any easier to talk to. She was very shy, Bella decided. She seemed to spend most of her break and lunchtimes reading on one of the benches in the playground. Bella had stopped to talk to her whenever she'd passed, but Sarah just wasn't all that chatty.

So the walk home from school was a little awkward. Mom did her best, asking Sarah about why they'd moved (because her mom had gotten a new job) and whether she liked her new apartment (yes, but she wished they had a yard). But it was hard to keep the conversation going, and Bella couldn't help wishing that she was back to being friends with

Megan again, and that it was Megan who was coming home to dinner instead.

As they walked into the front yard, the sound of barking greeted them. "I can hear Sid," Mom said, laughing. "He can always tell we're coming, Sarah. He gets all excited—it's nice. Although I have to say, he's far more excited when it's Bella or Tom coming than he is for me!"

Sarah nodded and she suddenly looked a lot less shy. "I can hear him, too," she said, laughing. "That squeaky noise! And a sort of scrabbling?"

Bella giggled. "He's trying to dig under the front door," she explained. "He always does it, even though you'd think by now he'd have figured out he never gets anywhere. Hey, Sid!"

Mom slid the key in the lock, and before they knew it Sid was waltzing happily on the front doorstep, dashing from Bella to Mom and back again. He sniffed at Bella and licked her fingers lovingly. Then he shot over to Mom to make sure she knew he loved her, too. He was so excited that it took him a few seconds to notice Sarah. But then he spotted her and went into his funny meeting-new-people pose.

"Oh, look, he did this when Gran came over!" Bella smiled at Sarah. "He gets all shy—watch him."

Sid put his head on one side and looked up quietly at Sarah, peering at her through his big white eyebrows and scraping one paw on the tiled doorstep.

"It's like he wants to ask you to dance, but he's not quite brave enough," Mom said, laughing. "Do you like dogs, Sarah?"

"I love them!" Sarah's eyes were sparkling, and she looked hopefully at Bella. "Is it OK if I pet him? Will he mind?"

"Oh no, he's really friendly," Bella said proudly. "Look, Sid, this is Sarah. He loves being tickled under the chin," she added.

Sarah crouched down and pet Sid, scratching him under the chin so his eyes closed blissfully, rubbing his ears, and then running her hand all down his spine so that he wriggled in delight.

"Wow, he loves that!" Bella said. She frowned at Sarah. "You're so good with him—but I thought you didn't have a dog?"

"I don't." Sarah looked up at her sadly. "But back at my old house we lived really close to my grandpa, and he has a gorgeous dog. Alfie. He's a collie mix. I used to go on walks with him and

Grandpa all the time."

"You must miss him," Bella said, thinking how much she would miss Sid, and she'd only had him a week. "Oh, and your grandpa, too, of course."

"Yeah." Sarah nodded sadly. "Grandpa emails me photos, but it's not the same."

"Come in, girls, you're still standing on the doorstep! What about something to drink?"

Somehow that made Bella and Sarah shy with each other again— Mom fussing around, asking Sarah if she'd like apple juice, and maybe a cookie? It showed how much they didn't know each other. Once they both had drinks, Bella took Sarah and Sid upstairs to her room.

Otherwise she had a feeling they'd sit at either end of the couch and not know what to say.

Sarah sat on the beanbag with Sid in front of her, eyeing her cookie.

"Don't get it anywhere near his nose," Bella warned her. "I'm training him, but he's not an angel. He loves cookies." She picked up a little tin from her desk. "Do you want to give him one of these? They're treats— they're supposed to be good for his teeth." She handed one of the little bone-shaped treats to Sarah and watched her feeding it to Sid.

Sid gobbled it down, and then flopped onto the floor, resting his nose on Sarah's feet, just in case she felt like giving him another treat.

"He really likes you," whispered Bella.

"I like him, too." Sarah glanced up at her shyly. "Thanks for letting me come over. I—I was a little surprised when you asked me. I mean, because you're friends with Megan and Lara and Chloe."

Bella shrugged. "Not at the moment I'm not. Megan's hardly spoken to me all week, and Lara was so horrible about Sid, I don't think I ever want to talk to her again."

Sarah shuddered. "I don't really like her. She . . . she just knows the absolute meanest thing to say. The best way to make people miserable."

Bella stared at her. "What did she say to you?" She'd never noticed Lara picking on Sarah.

Sarah shrugged, hunching up her shoulders. "Stuff about how I'd never have any friends here," she muttered. "And Megan asked why didn't I go back to my old school."

"Megan did?" Bella murmured, feeling shocked.

"Yeah. That's why I was so surprised when you asked me over. I thought you were like them." Sarah looked at her sideways and added, "Sorry."

"I don't like Lara and Chloe much, either. Megan isn't usually like that, though..." Bella nibbled her thumbnail.

"Well, she is sometimes," she admitted. "But she's fun, too. And most of the time she's nice." She sighed. "Anyway, why did you stick up for me, if you thought I was like Lara?" she asked suddenly.

Sarah grinned at her. "I wasn't sticking up for you. I was sticking up for Sid. And I thought that anybody who was so excited about getting a dog had to have some good points."

"Thanks!" Bella rolled her eyes, and Sarah let out a snort of laughter. This made Bella laugh, too, and then they couldn't stop.

Sid looked up at them both, blinking sleepily, and wondering why they were making so much noise. He sighed and snuggled back onto Sarah's feet.

"Are you really entering Sid into a dog show?" Sarah asked a few minutes later, when they'd just about stopped giggling.

Bella made a face. "I don't know. I only said it because I was so angry with Megan. She was being such a show-off, saying Coco was better than Sid. I didn't even think about what I was saying." She sighed. "She's never going to let me forget about it, you know. She was talking at lunchtime today about the dog show Coco's going to.

About how her dad's entered Coco in the puppy class. And then she looked at me and smiled . . ."

"But you *could* enter Sid into a dog show, too, you know," Sarah said, looking at her excitedly. "Grandpa took Alfie to one once, and it had fun contests, like catch the treat. Alfie won that. He got a ribbon and everything."

"Really?" Bella looked at her hopefully. "Maybe there's a show like that we could take Sid to. I bet he'd be *excellent* at catching treats."

Sid's ears twitched, then he looked up eagerly and bounced to his feet. Treat was a word he knew.

"See?" Bella started to laugh again, and Sid lay back down with a sigh. He didn't think they had any treats at all.

Chapter Six

The girls went downstairs to borrow Bella's mom's computer to find out if there was a dog show nearby that they could go to.

"Oh, look, click on that one! That's in Lace Hill, not far away," Sarah pointed out excitedly.

"Yes!" Bella opened up the page, and the two girls peered at it eagerly.

**Lace Hill Dog Club
Annual Show**

Open Show
Novelty Contests
Agility Display
Stalls
Refreshments
Fun Day Out for the Whole Family!

Saturday, March 22

"That's in a couple of weeks," Bella said thoughtfully. "I bet it's the same one Megan's entering Coco in. She said it was two weeks from Saturday."

"What does 'Open Show' mean?" Sarah asked, frowning.

"It means that any dog can enter— they don't have to have won a show somewhere else already," a voice came from behind them.

Bella and Sarah jumped—they hadn't heard Bella's dad come in, even though Sid was happily sniffing at him. They'd been too busy looking at the website.

"Oh . . . How did you know that, Dad?" asked Bella.

"I've been to that show before—years ago, Bella, before you were born. Mom and I went with your gran. They're right, it's a great day out! Some people take it very seriously, though."

"But there are fun contests, too," Bella said. "It says so. Sarah was telling me about a show she'd been to where the dogs had to catch treats. It sounded great!"

Her dad laughed and pointed to the computer. "Click on the novelty contests. It should tell you what they are."

Bella clicked where her dad had pointed. The screen flashed up with another page.

"'Waggiest tail'—oh, Sid could win that!" Bella giggled as she read down the list of contests. She turned to look at Sid, who was leaning against Dad's legs and gazing up at him adoringly. Dad had taken to giving him a treat when he came in from work, and Sid wasn't going to let him forget. His fluffy, feathery tail was sweeping back and forth across the carpet.

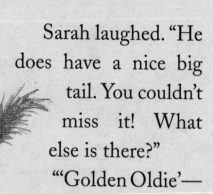

Sarah laughed. "He does have a nice big tail. You couldn't miss it! What else is there?"

"'Golden Oldie'—oh, that's for older dogs, of course. 'Prettiest Female,' 'Most Handsome Dog' . . ." Bella looked thoughtfully at Sid. "Well. Maybe not. But he could definitely enter this one—listen! 'Dog that the judges would most like to take home'!"

"It says no dogs under six months can compete at the show," Sarah said. "But Sid's older than that, isn't he?"

"I think so." Bella looked around at Dad questioningly. "They weren't exactly sure at the shelter."

"He's definitely more than six months, Bella, don't worry," said Dad. "Is this the show that you said Megan was entering?" he asked. "Isn't her dog very little? I guess she might just have turned six months old by the time of the show—it's not for another couple of weeks, after all."

Bella nodded. "So, Dad . . . Would you take me and Sid to the show? Pleeeaase?"

Dad grinned. "I think we should all go. Maybe you could come with us, Sarah. If your mom would let you."

Sarah looked delighted. "I'll ask her. So, which contests do you think you'll enter, Bella?"

Bella frowned at the computer. "I like the idea of 'Best Trick.' Except

Sid doesn't have one . . . But we've got two weeks to learn. I could teach him a trick. I bet I could!"

"Oh, I watched that group at the dog show I went to with Grandpa and Alfie!" said Sarah.

"What sort of tricks did the dogs do?" Bella asked anxiously. She wasn't sure she could teach Sid anything really complicated.

"A couple of dogs did a trick where their owners put a treat down right in front of them. Then they had to wait to eat it until their owners gave a signal."

Bella looked at Sid doubtfully. That sounded hard. Sid loved his treats. She couldn't imagine him leaving one uneaten.

"The dog that won stood on her hind

legs and walked across the field," Sarah said, frowning as she tried to remember. "Oh, and then at the end, her owner kind of leaned back and stretched his leg out, and she ran up his leg so he could hug her! But she was tiny—she was a King Charles spaniel. I think it would be hard for Sid to do that part. I bet he could walk on his hind legs, though. You'd just need to hold a treat up for him."

Bella looked hopefully at Sarah. "Do you want to come into the yard and see if we can get him to stand up?"

Dad laughed. "If this involves dog treats, it's going to be his new favorite game!"

Because it had been Sarah's idea to teach Sid how to walk on his hind legs, it seemed only fair to let her share in his training. Besides, even though Bella hadn't been looking forward to Sarah coming to her house, they'd ended up having a really good time. Sarah might be quiet, and not at all like Megan, but she was funny, and Bella liked her a lot.

Over the next two weeks they met up a couple of times to go to the park and practice Sid's special trick. Sarah's mom came with them. She said that Sid was the funniest thing she had ever seen. She thought he was bound to win. Sarah came to dinner the next Friday as well, and they had another practice session in the yard.

Bella was working at home with

Sid, too, although she had made her mom and dad and Tom promise not to watch them in the yard—she wanted Sid's trick to be a surprise. So of course when she got to school, she couldn't wait to update Sarah on how they were doing—which meant that they spent a lot of time chatting to each other in the corner of the playground, and laughing at whatever silly thing had happened the night before.

That morning, they were giggling together all over again. As they hurried into the closet to hang their coats up, Bella heard an upset sort of yelp behind her, and she swung around in surprise. Sarah was in the doorway, holding her arm, and Megan was next to her. Her old friend looked guilty.

"What did you do, Megan?" Bella demanded. "Sarah, are you OK?"

"Yeah, I just banged my arm . . ."

"You mean *she* banged it!" Bella snapped. "Did Megan shove you into the door, Sarah? You did, didn't you?" she said, turning angrily to Megan. "What was that for?"

"It was an accident." Megan shrugged, but she didn't look very convincing.

"Yeah, right! Come on, Sarah. We'll ask Mr. Peters for an ice pack. Don't let Megan get to you." Bella looked at Megan, skulking miserably by the door, and suddenly realized what was going on. "You're jealous," she gasped, with surprise in her voice. It was true, she was sure.

"What, of you?" Megan was trying to sound snotty, but she only managed to sound as though she was about to cry.

"You're jealous because I'm friends with someone else," said Bella. "Why don't you go and hang around with Lara and Chloe." She shook her head, but as she walked with Sarah down the hall to their classroom, she glanced back. Megan was actually crying.

Bella felt bad. She had been friends with Megan for years. Even though Megan was being totally horrible, she still couldn't help worrying about her.

Chapter Seven

Bella knew that she should talk to Megan, but Megan had said such mean things about Sid and about Sarah, too. She had started it all so Bella thought it should be up to her to make friends again. She didn't sit at the same table as Megan in class, so it wasn't as if they had to talk to each other. Bella just had to keep out of her way.

And as it turned out, she managed to get as far as the day of the dog show without saying anything to Megan at all. It definitely was the Lace Hill Show that Megan and Coco were going to—Bella had heard her telling Lara more about it.

Bella and Dad had decided that they would just go for three contests—"Waggiest Tail," "Dog the Judges Would Most Like to Take Home," and "Best Trick."

Sarah was coming with them to the show, so her mom dropped her off after breakfast. She had a bag with her, and she looked excited. "How's Sid? Is he nervous?" she asked.

Bella shook her head. "No, he's fast asleep in the kitchen. He doesn't have a clue what's going on. I am, though. I'm sure he's going to do something awful, like pee on the judge's leg, or something. What's in the bag?"

"Just my purse—Mom said there might be fun stalls to look at. I can't wait!"

Mom came into the hallway. "Hello, Sarah! We'd better hurry, girls. You want to get there and see what's going on before it starts, don't you? And we've got to get Sid into his travel crate—you know how long that takes."

Bella made a face.

"Doesn't he like it?" Sarah asked.

"He goes all silly and wriggly as soon as he sees it, but I think it's more that he's excited about going to places. So far he's only been to the woods in the car, and he loves it there, so it makes him a little hyper."

They walked out of the front door, and Dad opened the car's trunk. Sid's ears seemed to go frizzier than ever, and he let out a string of excited yelps before whirling around and around on the end of his leash, nearly tripping Bella.

"See?" Bella sighed. "I hope he doesn't get this excited at the show."

"I've got a secret weapon to get him in there." Dad sprinkled a few dog treats on the floor of the travel crate. "Hey, Sid, look!"

Sid sniffed, and jumped straight into the travel crate. He sat, gazing out of the window and panting happily as they set off. He loved the car—and his crate now smelled deliciously of chicken-flavored treats.

"Gosh, it's really big. . ." Bella murmured nervously. "So many people."

"And dogs. Oh, look at that gorgeous weiner dog! In that lady's bag, look!"

Sarah pointed at the lady walking past, whose bag had a head sticking out one end, and a tail at the other. "We need to find the registration tent and put Sid's name down."

Mom set off toward a white tent, and the others hurried after her. Bella and Sarah couldn't keep up—Sid wanted to stop and sniff everything.

"Bella, look! There's Megan," Sarah whispered, and Bella looked round.

"Oh, wow. And that's Coco. She really is cute."

Megan was standing by one of the fenced-off rings with her dad, and Coco on her pink leash. Coco looked beautiful, with her shiny golden coat and sparkly collar, but she was dancing about, and a couple of times she almost tripped people. Megan had to keep pulling her back and apologizing, and her dad looked annoyed.

"Coco, sit!" Megan hissed, but Coco wasn't listening at all.

Bella looked down at Sid proudly. He was naughty sometimes—especially about getting in the car—but now he was walking beautifully by her side.

Bella's dad waved to Megan, and she stared back at him, looking embarrassed. But the two dads didn't know that Bella and Megan weren't talking, and they started chatting, while Coco sniffed at Sid in a friendly sort of way.

Sid looked up at Bella, not quite sure what he was supposed to do. He hadn't met many other dogs since he'd left the shelter.

Bella patted him. "Good boy. Coco's just saying hello."

But Megan scowled and hauled Coco away from Sid, walking farther down the fenced ring, with Coco pulling back on her leash all the way.

Bella looked at Sarah and shrugged her shoulders.

Bella's dad raised his eyebrows at Bella and told Megan's dad they'd better go and register for the competition.

"Why was Megan so rude to you? What was all that about?" he asked Bella as soon as they were out of earshot.

Bella shrugged, embarrassed, and Sarah explained for her.

"Megan and Lara were making jokes about Sid being odd, and not a pedigree dog like Coco. But did you see Coco getting into trouble? Sid's way better behaved, Bella. You should be proud of him."

"I noticed Coco messing around, too," Dad agreed. "Anyway, I'm sure you and Megan can work it out, Bella—you've known each other such a long time."

"I know." Bella sighed. "But it wasn't just Sid she was mean about, Dad. She's been horrible to Sarah, too. Oh, I'll talk to her. But not today."

"Are you all right?" Sarah whispered as Bella stood at the edge of the ring.

"Just a little nervous," Bella gulped. "I'm glad it's 'Best Trick' first. I'm not so worried about the others. I hope Sid isn't scared by all the noise, though—we should have gotten Tom to play the guitar or something while we were practicing."

"He'll be great, you both will. Oh, I think it's your turn."

Bella heard her name called, and she grinned nervously at Mom, Dad, Tom, and Sarah, who had really good places at the front to watch.

"And this is Bella Pascoe, with her mixed-breed, Sid! And he really is a character—look at him!" The announcer sounded as though he was trying not to laugh, and Bella looked down at Sid in surprise. He didn't seem to be at all worried about the audience.

Sid could hear people clapping and laughing and he glanced around the ring. This was nice! Lots of people were looking at him. He stepped out smartly, his tail swishing and his ears pricked at a jaunty angle.

Bella stopped in the middle of the ring and Sid looked up at her with hopeful eyes. He could smell that she had treats. He hoped they were going to do the walking on his hind paws—that meant lots of treats. It was his favorite game.

"Come on, Sid, up!" Bella said, holding a treat over his nose, and Sid stood up at once. The treat was just a little higher than his nose, but he knew Bella would give it to him in a minute. He skittered across the ring, and looked around in surprise as everybody started clapping.

"Good boy! And again." Bella led him back across the ring, and this time they stopped in the middle to do a twirl, which made the audience laugh. The laughter was very loud, but it was a good noise and Sid panted happily. Just the last bit now, and then he was pretty sure Bella would give him the whole handful of treats. He watched carefully, waiting for Bella to pat her knees.

If he did it too soon, Bella might fall over—that had happened once in the yard.

"Come on, Sid!" Bella patted her knees, and Sid launched himself at her joyfully, leaping into her arms for the big finish.

"Well done!" Bella whispered in his ear as she fed him all the chicken-flavored treats, and listened to everybody clapping. "You were great. But you'd better not get any fatter, Sid, or we won't be able to do that last part . . ."

"He looks so good with a blue ribbon on his collar," Sarah said admiringly. "He should have another one for the 'Dog the Judges Would Most Like to Take

Home,' though. You were robbed!"

Bella shrugged. "I knew there was no way he was going to beat that golden retriever," she said, munching her sandwich and trying to ignore Sid, who was doing his best impression of a prizewinning dog who had never, ever been fed. "That was the sappiest dog I've ever seen."

"Even more lovey-dovey than Sid when he wants sandwiches," Dad agreed. "No, Sid. Not even for a champion blue-ribbon winner." He chuckled to himself. "I still can't believe you kept all of his tricks a secret, Bella. It was amazing."

Mom nodded. "I was so proud of you. Oh, it's almost time for the 'Waggiest Tail' contest."

Bella hauled Sarah up off the picnic blanket, and Mom passed them Sid's leash.

Bella looked thoughtfully at Sarah as they walked across to the ring. Her friend kept looking longingly at all the dogs they went past. Bella hadn't realized until now how much Sarah must be missing her grandpa's dog. "Do you want to take Sid for this contest?" she asked suddenly. "I know it's not the same as having Alfie, but I think you should. You worked on training him, too. And it was you who suggested we should look for a show with fun contests!"

"Can I really?" Sarah asked, her eyes shining excitedly.

Bella nodded. "Definitely. Sid loves you, so it won't bother him. Look, it's that same nice lady calling out the names. I'll explain to her—I'm sure she won't mind."

Bella pushed the leash into Sarah's hand and hurried over to the lady sitting in the corner of the ring to explain. She could see Sarah crouching next to Sid and petting him lovingly, so she was sure she'd done the right thing.

Bella dashed back. "She says it's fine," she told Sarah. "The competition is about to start—come on. Over here." Bella pushed Sarah into the right place in the line of dogs, and watched proudly as they all walked into the ring.

"Where's Sid?" Tom asked, looking around worriedly as he and Mom and Dad came over.

"I let Sarah take him," Bella said. "You don't mind, do you? You did say you didn't want to be in the show."

Tom shuddered. "I definitely don't mind. Sid looks like he loves all the attention, but I'd hate it."

When it was Sarah and Sid's turn Sarah rubbed the perfect spot on Sid's spine, and he wagged his tail so hard he nearly fell over.

"And we have a clear winner there," called the announcer. "Yes, the judges are going for Sid! Handled by one of his best friends—Sarah! Well done, Sid and Sarah!"

Chapter Eight

Bella jumped up and down, clapping, and Sarah hurried back to her with scarlet cheeks, clutching another blue ribbon. "You won!" Bella hugged her. "You see, I knew I was right to get you to go in. Sid's a champion. Two firsts!"

"What's the next contest, Bella?" Tom asked. "Whatever it is, I think your friend Megan's in it." He pointed across the ring to where Megan was lining up with Coco. "Oh, 'Cutest Puppy Under Nine Months.' Well, she is cute. She doesn't look very happy about it, though."

Coco was pulling, and pawing at her leash, as though she wanted to get away. Megan was trying to calm her down, but she looked worried, too, and Coco was whimpering.

"Poor thing, I don't think she likes how noisy it is," Bella said anxiously. "Oh no!"

Coco had been pulling and scrabbling at her collar so much, and now she slipped right out of it. She stood there for a second, looking bewildered by her sudden freedom and the noise. Megan tried to grab her, but a little boy screamed because he'd dropped his ice cream, and Coco shot away with a squeak. She bolted along the side of the ring toward Bella and Sarah, and then darted out through a forest of feet and off into the rest of the field.

"Coco!" Megan wailed, dashing after her, but she was blocked by all the other handlers and dogs going into the ring.

"We have to help catch her!" Bella gasped. "Look after Sid, Sarah." She pushed and squeezed her way through the crowd of people and looked around anxiously for Coco.

The little spaniel was cowering by the side of an ice-cream van, obviously terrified. Bella walked over to her, trying to be slow and gentle—she really wanted to grab Coco before she ran off again, but if she moved too fast, she'd just frighten her away.

"Dog treats!" Bella gasped, realizing she still had half the pack in her pocket. "Hey, Coco . . . Look what I've got." She held out a few, rattling them gently and murmuring some soothing words to the nervous little spaniel. "Pretty girl, yes, look. Yummy treats. Pretty Coco, come on now . . ."

Coco eyed her worriedly, but she could smell the treats, and the girl's voice was gentle, not mad. She wanted

Megan, but she was frightened of all the noise, and she didn't dare go back and find her. She crept slowly forward and sniffed at Bella's hand, and then she started to nibble at the crunchy treats.

Bella ran a gentle hand over Coco's head, still murmuring soothing words, and then, as the puppy munched the last of the treats, Bella picked her up.

Coco wriggled a little, but Bella was holding her carefully, tight enough that she couldn't squirm away.

"We need to find Megan, and your collar," she whispered. "Hey, look, Coco, there she is!"

Megan was racing toward them, with tears running down her cheeks. As soon as Coco saw her, she wriggled eagerly, stretching out of Bella's arms to reach her. Megan hugged her, and Coco licked her chin, and nuzzled at her neck. Bella laughed—Coco might not like the dog show, but it was obvious she adored Megan.

"I thought I'd never find her!" Megan said gratefully, looking at Bella. "You must have run after her really fast. I was worried she might get into the parking lot." She shuddered, and Bella put an arm around her shoulders.

"It's OK, we got her back. Here, let's put her collar on again." Bella helped Megan fasten it, and Bella put Coco down gently. Then she glanced back up at Megan.

"I'm really sorry I agreed with Lara about Sid," Megan said. "I was so horrible. And to Sarah, too. It's just, I never thought we wouldn't be friends, and then suddenly you were with *her* all the time . . ."

"She's nice. A lot nicer than Lara and Chloe," Bella said. "I still like you, but I don't want to hang around with them anymore."

Megan looked at her feet. "I know. I don't like them much either. But if you aren't friends with Lara, she says bad things about you . . ."

Bella shrugged. "I don't care." And she didn't, she realized. She probably would, when Lara started up again, but she would tell herself that it didn't really matter. "We can just walk away," she pointed out to Megan.

"I guess so. I'll say sorry to Sarah." Megan looked at her hopefully. "Do you think we can go back to being friends?"

Bella smiled. "We could try . . ."

"How did you get Sid to do that amazing walking on his hind paws?" Megan asked, as they wandered along the path through the park.

It was Sunday afternoon, and Bella had arranged for her and Megan and Sarah and their moms to meet up. She was a bit worried about Megan and Sarah not getting along, so she wanted them to try and get to know each other before they all had to go back to school on Monday.

"You saw that?" Bella asked, feeling pleased. "It's all about dog treats. Sid's really greedy. He'd do anything for them."

"I wonder if Coco could." Megan sighed. "She's cute, but I'm not very good at getting her to do what she's told."

"She's little," Sarah pointed out. "She'll probably get better as she gets older."

"Maybe . . . But I wish she'd hurry up," Megan sighed. "She keeps eating things. One of my mom's shoes yesterday."

"Why don't you bring her to the dog-training classes at the center?" Bella suggested. "We're starting to go next week."

Megan looked hopeful. "That's a good idea. Is the class OK for beginners, too? I mean, Sid's already so good."

Bella glowed. He *was* good. He was great, actually. "I'm sure it's all right," she agreed proudly, watching Sid and Coco walking sweetly next to each other.

"They look like friends already," Sarah said, laughing at them. "Look, they're chatting."

Bella looked over. It was true. Sid and Coco were standing with their heads together, watching a jogger speeding down the path toward them. They looked so cute next to each other.

"I don't think they like his orange sneakers," Megan whispered, and Bella tried not to laugh. It felt good, being with Megan and Sarah. And Coco and Sid obviously loved walking together, too.

"They're definitely friends," Bella said, smiling at Megan. She didn't need to say it, but what she really meant was, *We all are . . .*

Read them all!

 Lost in the Snow

 Lost in the Storm

 Sam the Stolen Puppy

 Alfie All Alone

 Max the Missing Puppy

 Sky the Unwanted Kitten

 Ginger the Stray Kitten

 Harry the Homeless Puppy

 Timmy in Trouble

 Ellie the Homesick Puppy

 Jess the Lonely Puppy

 Buttons the Runaway Puppy

 Oscar's Lonely Christmas

 Alone in the Night

 Misty the Abandoned Kitten

 Lucky the Rescued Puppy

 Whiskers the Lonely Kitten

 Lucy the Littlest Puppy

 Smudge the Stolen Kitten

 Cookie the Deserted Puppy

 The Kidnapped Kitten

 The Frightened Kitten